Text and illustrations copyright © 2012 Seymour Chwast
Published in 2012 by Creative Editions   P.O. Box 227, Mankato, MN 56002 USA
Creative Editions is an imprint of The Creative Company
Printed in Italy
Library of Congress Cataloging-in-Publication Data
Chwast, Seymour.
Bobo's smile / by Seymour Chwast.
Summary: Depressed by the closure of the circus, a clown named Bobo embarks on an
assortment of adventures around the world, but he is not able to smile again until
returning to his home and work.
ISBN 978-1-56846-221-9
1. Adventure and adventurers—Juvenile literature. 2. Clowns—Juvenile literature. I. Title.
G525.C536 2012   [E]—dc22   2011010831
CPSIA: 081111 PO1497

First edition 9 8 7 6 5 4 3 2 1

My name is Bobo.

One day,
they closed
the circus.

I felt sad.

I went on rides.

I saw strange buildings.

I rode an elephant.

I visited
new cities.

I went underwater in a submarine.

The buttons fell off my clothes.

So I started to juggle them.

I smiled.

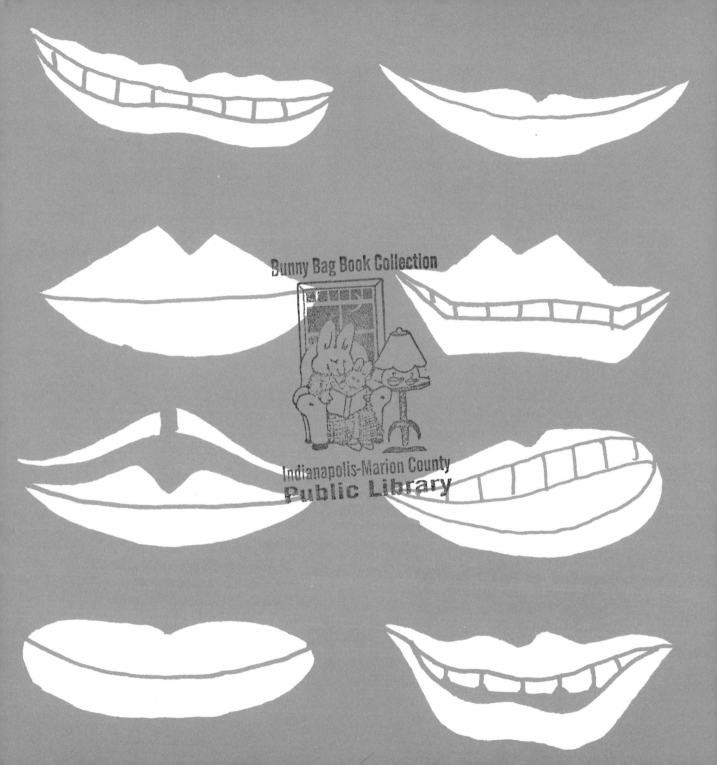